Dedicated to all children

To those who find themselves, like Rainbow, last in many things they attempt.

To those, like Rainbow, who are impatient and don't want to wait until the best time.

Finally to those who deal with pride, because they are the ones who always are the best!

-Mary

www.mascotbooks.com

Rainbow Deals with Pride

For more information, please contact:

Mascot Books
560 Herndon Parkway #120
Herndon, VA 20170
info@mascotbooks.com

Library of Congress Control Number: 2015903480

CPSIA Code: PRT0515A
ISBN-13: 978-1-63177-144-6

Printed in the United States

Rainbow Deals with Pride

Written by
Mary Clark Dalton

Illustrated by **Stacy Moody**

Life was changing quickly for Rainbow. Butterflies came from near and far just to get a glimpse of his beautiful wings.

One change Rainbow did not notice, however, was the change in his attitude. It seemed as though he was always admiring himself in the mirror. *My! I am one good-looking butterfly!* Rainbow thought.

Instead of hiding from all the other butterflies as he did before, Rainbow was constantly seeking them out, spreading his wings as far as he could for all to see. He could not get enough of their praise—and their envy. He especially liked finding Lightning, the one who had taunted Rainbow mercilessly when he was still a caterpillar.

Who's laughing now? Rainbow thought with a smile. *He might be fast, but my large wings move more air, so I always win the races now. Speaking of races, where is he anyway? I'm in the mood for a good one!*

"Oh, Lightning, where are you?" Rainbow called. Looking around, he noticed a group of butterflies around a large patch of flowers. There in the middle was Lightning. Suddenly, all the butterflies started to fly away. *Hmm that's odd*, Rainbow thought. *I wonder where they're going in such a hurry.*

"Hey, Lightning, wait! You want to race?" Rainbow asked, trying to catch up.

"Oh grow up, Rainbow," said Lightning. "There's more to life than races and showing off."

"You didn't think that when *you* were winning," snapped Rainbow.

"Harrumph," huffed Lightning as he flew out of sight.

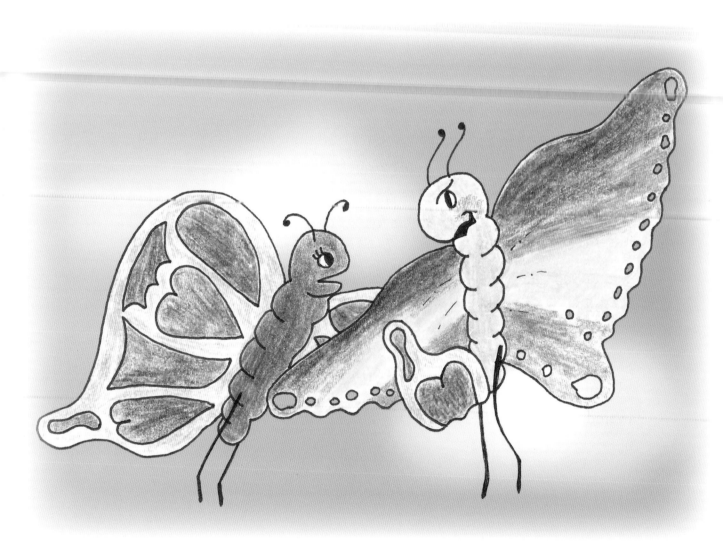

He's just jealous like all the others, thought Rainbow. *Who needs them anyway? I'm sure there are plenty of other butterflies who would love to spend time with the largest, most beautiful butterfly around.*

Rainbow decided to practice his flying, and he made sure he was where other butterflies could see him. He was just about to make another loop when he felt a nudge on his wing. *Who would be bold enough to nudge me?*

Rainbow turned around sharply, ready for a confrontation, when he noticed a familiar wing. "Mom! What are you doing here?"

"I should ask *you* that question," replied Mom.

Rainbow didn't want his mom to find out what he was really doing, so he answered, "Oh, I'm just practicing my flying."

"Yes, I saw you practicing," said Mom, "but to me it looked more like you were showing off."

Rainbow hung his head. He knew he couldn't deny it. "Oh, Mom," sighed Rainbow, "I was just having a little fun!"

"Fun? Is that what it felt like when you were being taunted?"

"No, Mom, it wasn't," said Rainbow. "I'm sorry."

But he wasn't really sorry. As soon as his mother was out of sight, he started flaunting his wings for all the butterflies to see. Only this time, instead of looking at him, they all flew away.

"Hey, where are you guys headed?" he shouted.

"Somewhere far away!" a few of them shouted back.

Rainbow became angry. "You're just jealous, because I am the strongest, most beautiful butterfly around!"

As Rainbow watched them leave, he felt a twinge of regret, but it left as quickly as it came. *Just as well*, he thought. *I better get busy and collect some pollen before I go home, or Mom's really going to be upset with me.*

Rainbow worked diligently for a while and then headed home. As he entered the house, his mother was waiting for him.

"I'm surprised you could get that head of yours through the door," Mom laughed.

"What do you mean?" Rainbow asked. Panicking, he ran to the mirror to take a look, afraid of what he would see. To his relief he looked as beautiful as ever.

His mother started giggling again.

"What's so funny?" Rainbow pouted.

"Oh, my sweet Rainbow, come here!" Mom said. Rainbow approached his mother reluctantly. "That's just an old saying," she said while stroking his beautiful wings. "It means you are proud and think too much of yourself."

"Mom, don't I have the right to be proud of the beautiful butterfly I have become?" Rainbow asked. "After all, it was a long time coming."

"Yes, Rainbow," Mom said. "But there are two kinds of pride one can have: the kind that makes you show off and think you're better than others, and the kind that lets you know you have more than others and inspires you to use those advantages for good."

Mom continued, "You see, Rainbow, all of us have special gifts, and we should use them for good and not bad. Then when we all work together, we have unity, and can accomplish much more. Think about the things your friends can do that you can't."

"Ha!" Rainbow said. "I am better at *everything*!"

"Everything?" his mom questioned. "If you think about it, I am sure you'll find a few things that others can do better than you."

Rainbow headed outside and started thinking about his friends. There was Lightning who was fast. *But I'm faster*, thought Rainbow. He had to admit though, the only reason he was faster than Lightning was because he had a larger wingspan. Plus, Lightning's smaller wings meant that he could get through smaller places than Rainbow could.

Rainbow thought of Snappy, who could remove pollen in a snap. There was Boulder, who was stronger than all the other butterflies. He thought of his friend Happy, who always had a funny joke to tell. Then there was Tiny, who was so small that Rainbow could carry her on his wing.

And what about Gracie? Rainbow couldn't help but smile when he thought of her. She flew so gracefully that it mesmerized him. All the boy butterflies hoped she would look their way. Some even did silly things to get her attention, but not Rainbow.

On and on he went, thinking about every butterfly he knew. To Rainbow's amazement, he realized the other butterflies could do a lot of things he couldn't. "Mom is always right," Rainbow said to himself.

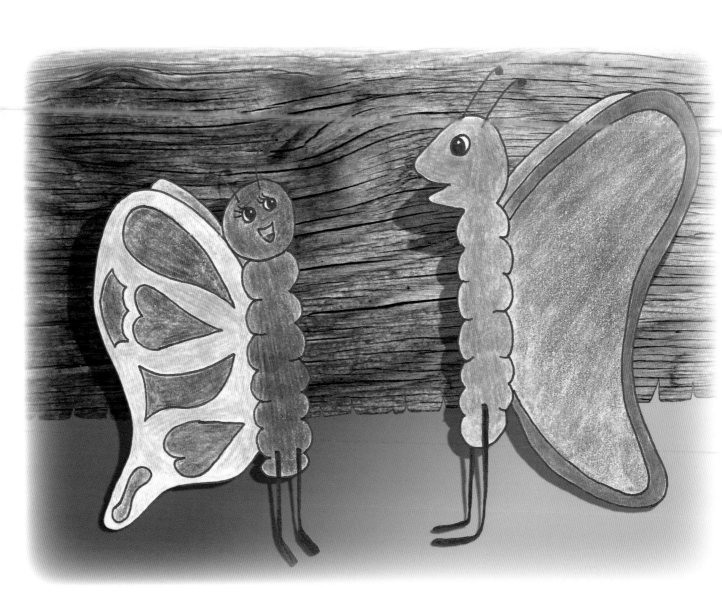

Rainbow went to tell his mom that she was right but when he stepped inside, he saw that she and Dad were deep in conversation. Rainbow heard his name and listened quietly.

"I'm worried about Rainbow," Mom told Dad.

"What do you mean?" Dad asked.

"Well, I caught up with Rainbow today when he was supposed to be doing his chores," said Mom, "but instead he was showing off in front of the other butterflies. He seemed to enjoy making the other butterflies feel small."

"What did you say to him?" asked Dad.

"I told him about pride and how it can be used for good and bad. I also told him to think of the things his friends can do better than he. That's what he's outside doing right now. I'm just worried that he might lose all his friends if he keeps this attitude. I've seen it happen before," Mom sighed.

"Well, I'll talk to him later," said Dad, "but I wouldn't worry too much. Rainbow has a good head on his wings. He knows what's right. He's just excited to finally be a butterfly."

"I guess you're right," said Mom. "I'll try to use some of that patience I'm always telling him about." As she turned to call Rainbow she noticed he had already come inside.

Rainbow cleared his throat and tried to speak, but the words would not come out. Rainbow wasn't quite sure what to say after what he'd heard. Deep down Rainbow knew that his parents were right, but it hurt to know they were disappointed in him.

His mother noticed the hurt on his face. "Rainbow, how long have you been listening?" Mom asked.

"Long enough," he said softly. "But it's okay, Mom. You're right. I've been acting proud and puffed-up lately. I'm sorry." This time, Rainbow really was sorry.

"Maybe I don't even deserve to be a butterfly. Maybe I should have stayed a caterpillar. I never do anything right," Rainbow sniffled.

"Now, Rainbow, that's not true," said his mom. "Remember how you helped Sniffy and Wanda? Think where they would be now if not for you."

Rainbow remembered how hard he'd worked to help his friends, and it did make him feel a little better. Still that was when he was a caterpillar not a butterfly.

"Mom, I'm just not good at being a butterfly," Rainbow sighed.

"Well, Rainbow, what did you do when you felt bad about being a caterpillar?" Mom asked.

"I looked for things I could do as a caterpillar that I could not do as a butterfly," Rainbow remembered.

All of a sudden, it was as if a light had turned on in Rainbow's head. He knew exactly what he had to do!

"I've got some things I need to do, Mom," he said. Rainbow headed outside with a smile on his face and a song in his heart. *A promise, a promise. A rainbow is a promise.*

"I do love that song!" Rainbow shouted as he flew high into the sky.

THE COLORS OF A RAINBOW

All the colors of a Rainbow did you ever wonder why?
Each color is so special and here's the reason why.
Each color is a promise, stretched out across the sky.
Just keep your eyes toward the heavens and look way, way up high
A promise, a promise the rainbow is a promise.
The sun is gonna shine again the clouds will never win!

Oh, rainbow, you're so special your colors too beautiful to say.
You always keep your promise the clouds have gone away.
The sun is shining down again you'll always save the day.
A rainbow is a promise to you that joy will be here to stay.
A promise, a promise the rainbow is a promise.
The sun is gonna shine again the clouds will never win!

Mary Clark Dalton lives in Stanleytown, Virginia with her husband, Keith. She has a great love for children and longs to help them learn to make the right decisions in life. She believes every child can reach their full potential with encouragement and leadership. It is her desire that through her stories, children will learn moral values that will stay with them the rest of their lives. This is Mary's third book in the *Rainbow* series, the first two being *Rainbow's Promise* and *Rainbow Learns to Fly*.

Coming soon...

Rainbow Learns the Golden Rule

Bonus Coloring Book!

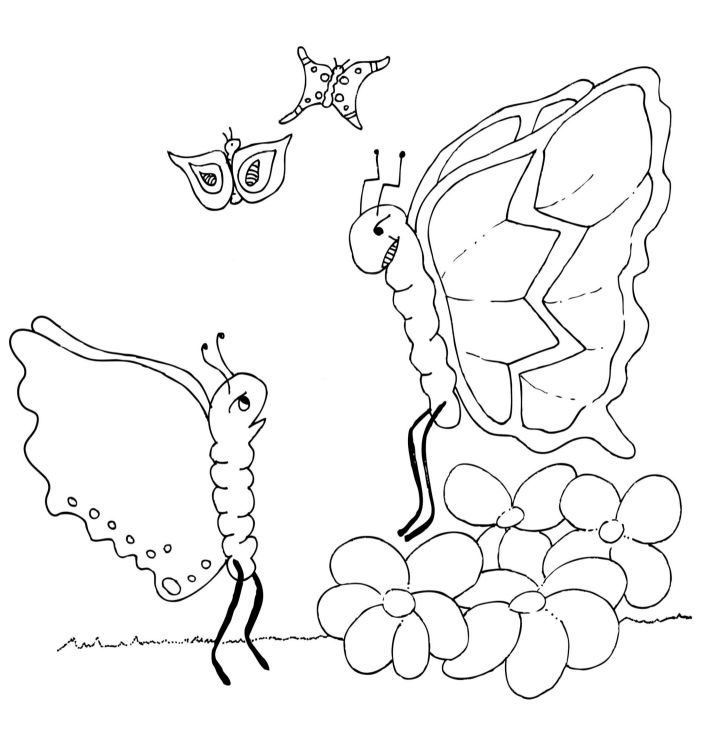

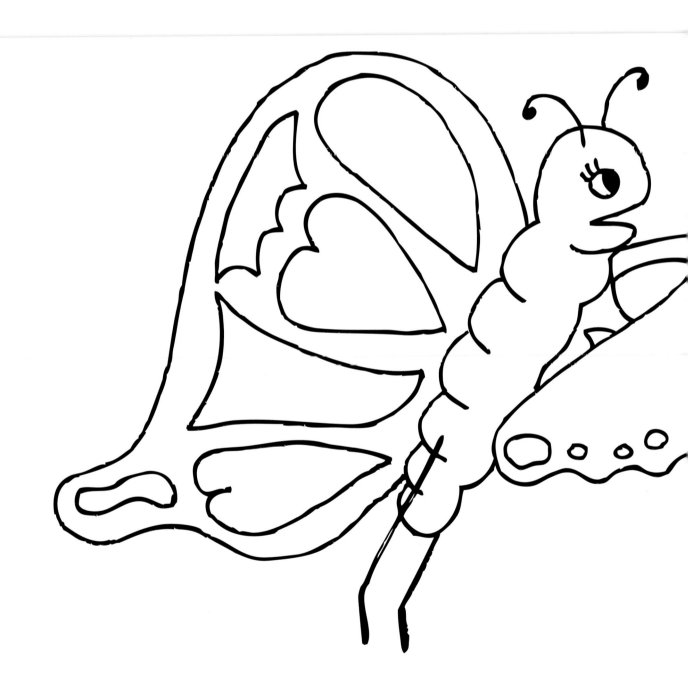

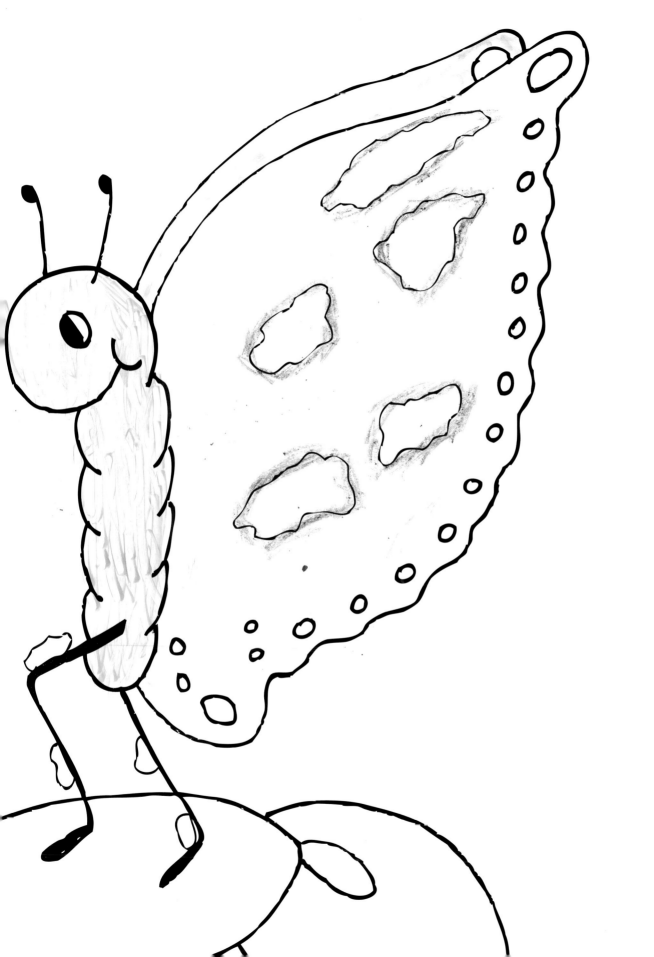

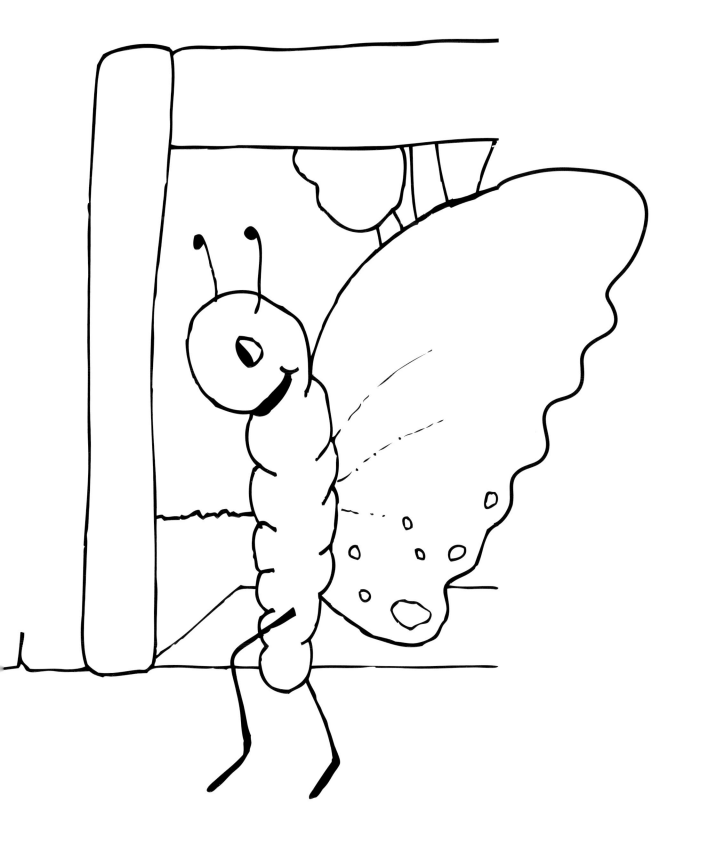

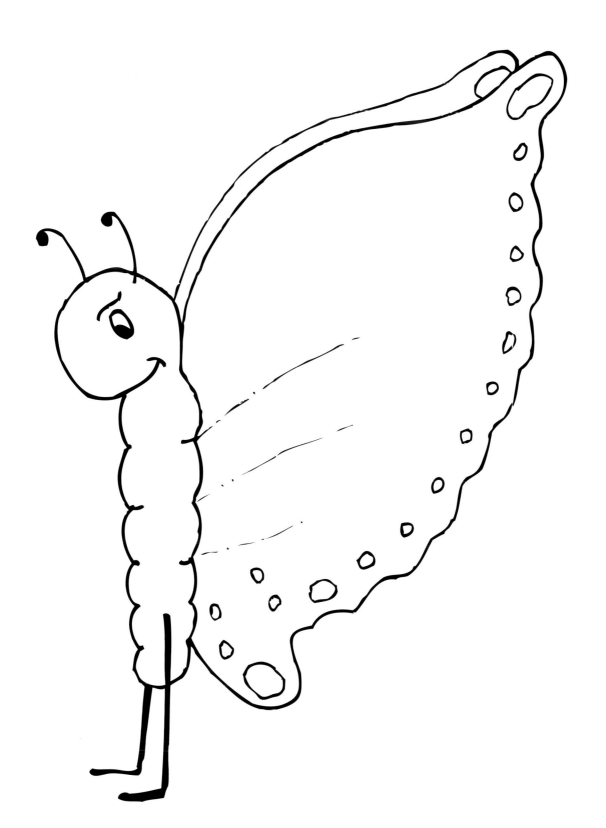